Copyright © 2021 by Jannette Quackenbush

ISBN-13: 978-1-940087-30-6

Table of Contents

The Old Buhrstone Quarries
*Along State Route 50 (at Peacock
Road) and the backroads between
McArthur, Ohio 45651
39.256858, -82.498965
To about Stone Quarry Road
39.234789, -82.423563*

Headless Peddler of Elk Fork

Downtown McArthur, built on the early buhrstone industry. In the center is one of the round millstones made from buhrstone.

In 1805, a miller named Musselman started a quarry after discovering buhrstone, a mix of flint, quartz, and limestone used to make millstones. It was on land between Chillicothe and Athens running beside Elk Fork, a tributary of Raccoon Creek. Right away, Musselman hired a man named Pierson, who later took over the business, built a cabin, and made the first permanent settlement.

A millstone quarry boomtown grew from the settlement consisting of about 50 families living and working in quarrying and making the millstones. The workers stripped the land, and the stone was extracted and pieced together to create a composite. The millstones became known as Raccoon buhrs as the quarries were located near Raccoon Creek. Strange things began to happen in the settlement after a few years. Travelers taking the path that led from Chillicothe through McArthur and then to Athens started getting accosted by a ghost. Locals heard horrid screams sweeping up from a certain place just off the road that led into a valley. Rumors began that a headless man stumbled awkwardly in the area around the quarries.

Old roads around the quarries.

John Dillon was a shoemaker in the late 1800s in McArthur. One evening a neighbor knocked on his door and asked Dillon to repair the soles on some boots. It took some time as it was late at night and he had to work by candlelight. When he was finished, Dillon bid the other man goodnight, and the neighbor went along his way in the darkness.

It was not long after the neighbor departed when the shoemaker was awakened by a loud thud and then a frantic pounding on the door. Dillon pushed himself from the bed to find the neighbor standing there shaking. He had been running so excitedly to the house that he had tripped on the steps and fallen. He told Dillon that after he set out, a woman appeared before him that was forty feet tall. When he tried to fend her off with blows, his fists went right through her body. She refused to allow him to pass.

Elk Fork—where ghosts were seen.

The ghostly tales could not be ignored. Even the skeptics who lived in the area knew what caused the haunting. A peddler often passed along that trail paralleling Elk Fork to visit the settlements on his route. Everyone knew him; he was quite a fetching sight to see as his face was framed in a 'throat whisker,' a heavy beard. He drove a new-fangled four -wheel buggy not seen before in the area filled with table cutlery, silver spoons, lace, and material for sewing, and special treats for children.

The peddler was quick to win over the quarry workers and their families with his wit and charm. He made himself so welcome that the peddling man was able to stay beneath the townspeople's roofs for a few nights while he sold his wares across the settlement, up and down the rugged hills from farm to farm. Then, quite suddenly, he disappeared as if the world swallowed him up.

A hunter following a doe in a deep ravine along the Chillicothe-Athens path happed upon a clump of brush and made a ghastly discovery. On one high ridge of the quarry where timbermen had cut a great oak, an ax had been left behind by a workman when cutting down the tree, and he had not yet returned to retrieve it. The brush had been heavily trampled, and there were bloodstains on the ground as if there had been a great fight. On the log was left a piece of throat with hair matching the peddler's whiskers.

Robbers must have ambushed the peddler and cut off his head with the ax, an easier route as one local offered —"they were afeard to shoot on account of the rifle crack—they've brained him. And to make sure of the job, they axed his head off." Later, they found the wheels of his buggy in the deep ravine.

**Alonzo Eckelberry's Route
Along Infirmary Road**
Zaleski, Ohio 45698
39.275497, -82.413221
To
39.272864, -82.443201

White Thing of Infirmary Road

Shry Hill on Infirmary Road where a man took a wild, ghostly ride.

Outside of Zaleski, an old gravel road weaves its way to the bustling town of McArthur. At one time, the Vinton County Infirmary and its little cemetery were settled on the path, and such those in the community called it Infirmary Road. Little farmsteads were spread far apart along its route, and between fields and meadows, there were long patches of deep, dark forest.

Most people avoided this little stretch of road after dusk. It had a ghost. Many reputable people talked about it long ago and retold that it followed them after dark. Alonzo Eckelberry was traveling the road from Zaleski on horseback one night in the late 1800s. Just as he passed the old Herrold's Mill along Racoon Creek and was in sight of a small homestead, he saw something white keeping pace beside him. When the man hastened his horse with a gentle tickle of his heels to ribs, the white thing sped up. When he slowed, it also matched the pace. As he passed the house, the specter jumped up on the back of the frightened man's horse.

Startled, Eckelberry turned his horse around to speed back to Zaleski. Looking backward, he could see the ghost perched atop the rear of his ride, but the horse appeared unaware. Then, when he got to a slope called Shry Hill for the family living at the peak, the ghost jumped off. Eckelberry lost no time in widening the expanse between himself and the horrifying apparition. And he refused, like many, to travel that route after dusk again.

Axtel Ridge
The Vinton Furnace State
Experimental Forest
Off Wolf Oak
Axtel Ridge
Hamden, Ohio 45634

Nightmares on Axtel Ridge

Tying a marker. Tiny fluorescent orange vinyl tape was supposed to mark my way back. But somehow, they kept 'falling' off.

Every one of us has those really bad nightmares, the ones awakening us in the middle of the night in a cold, dripping sweat with heart hard-thumping like the frenzied, frantic beating of sticks to a marching band's drums during halftime at a high school football game. Getting chased. Falling. Being alone. Ghosts. Handfuls of bugs crawling on you. What is your worst fear reflected in your dreams?

Well, mine is getting lost—that world-spinning anxiety when I cannot retrace my last steps, or I cannot remember the direction of my previous jeep turn at an intersection of a road. I always have double GPS running for my rough country adventures. But when I am out and about foot hiking a backwoods trail, it is just me, my unpredictable cellphone, and my stupidly poor sense of direction. Sometimes, when the trees and brush are thick and there is no visible trail, I bring a roll of fluorescent orange vinyl tape. I rip a section off the roll and tie ribbons to limbs like tens of tiny streamers marking my way back to an easier-to-follow path, pulling each with relief on my return.

I am sure you are wondering where I am going with this, so I will get to the point. I was on the trail to find an old ghost story at one of southeastern Ohio's Division of Forestry experimental areas. It has over 12,000 acres to get lost in, but I had my cellphone with two different mapping systems; although deep in the hollows, the little locator button jumps around and can be fickle at best. Thus, I also had my roll of bright orange vinyl tape. After three separate days of hiking the ridges and creeks, old roads, and hunter trails, I finally found what I was looking for—the place the old house once stood. The home is nearly gone. Prickly briers, thorny blackberry, poison ivy, and ancient planted pines have almost taken over the old property—the structure is nothing more than ruins tucked on a hillock at the edge of an overgrown ridge.

In the 1920s, though, it was part of the Axtel Ridge farming property of 65-year-old farmer William (Bill) Stout and his second wife, 58-year-old Sarah, and home to 34-year-old Arthur, a son from Bill's previous marriage. Bill and Sarah had been married around twenty years, and she had helped raise Arthur since he was around 13-years-old.

Sarah was probably not thrilled Arthur made a home nearby. There was friction between the two, enflamed by disagreements here and there. They were two different souls. She was older, modest, and virtuous—perhaps a bit too much at times. Arthur was younger and could be indifferent, callous, and incorrigible —maybe a bit too much at times also.

The home on Axtel Ridge. Image: Vinton County Historical Society-Alice's House.

Of course, the community chatter and gossip centering around Arthur's improprieties did not improve the stepmother's and stepson's rocky relationship. It was just the opposite. Although highly respected among friends and neighbors, the Stouts had fallen prey to a few of the gossiping sort. In the spring of that year, Arthur had settled down in this little, four-room house on his father's land.

Along with him, he had brought a young woman, Inez Palmer, who was, by his accounts, hired to live in the home to do housework and help care for his sons—9-year-old William and 13-year-old Artie. Stepmother Sarah knew better, and so too did the locals. The matter escalated because the petite dark-haired, brown-eyed beauty, not much taller than five feet and weighing little more than a hundred pounds, appeared scandalously young.

It was evident that there was more to the relationship than Arthur had alluded. Sarah was a God-fearing woman, and enough so, she told her stepson the illicit behavior had to stop immediately. "Lasciviously associating and cohabiting in sin together" at the time was still illegal and could potentially land a couple in jail. Arthur snickered at his stepmother's request and refused. Humbled and filled with righteousness, Sarah stomped down to the local justice of the peace and had him arrested in November of 1926 for cohabitating with the woman. His father, a less-rigid and peaceable man, believed jailing Arthur was too harsh a punishment. He hired a lawyer, and the court released Arthur on bond. Sarah remarked to a neighbor she feared greatly for her life after the release of her stepson.

Her apprehension was not unwarranted. A few days later, on November 17th, 1926, 14-year-old Manuel Perry was sent to Bill Stout's home, not far from Arthur's house, running an errand for his mother. When nobody answered the front door, he strolled innocently to the parlor door. He came across a terrifying scene—the bitter reek of burnt flesh hit his nostrils, and before his eyes lay a gruesome mix of blood and charred skin. Sarah Stout was lying face down on the linoleum floor near the kitchen stove—savagely beaten, and her clothing and head burned.

Maude Collins was the sheriff of Vinton County at the time, taking over the position after her husband, Sheriff Fletcher Collins, was shot at close range by a 12-gauge shotgun in 1925, issuing an arrest warrant to George Steele for speeding. On the day they found Sarah dead, she and her deputy arrived at the scene to find Bill Stout sitting on the porch steps and sobbing uncontrollably. It was not difficult to see that whoever had murdered the poor woman had waited for her to be alone and had made her feel secure enough to turn her back to her killer as there was a horrible blow to the rear of her head.

The murder was coldblooded and calculated. Her usually easy-going husband was hardly a suspect, and his alibi, picking corn far in the fields, was corroborated. Perhaps the killer had toyed with the woman, working up a casual conversation before being invited into the house. It did not take long for an investigation to lead to Arthur Stout. It was not simply because bloodhounds ran from Arthur Stout's home directly to Bill Stout's kitchen. The dogs had howled and bayed, following the path the son had said he dragged a wagon tongue on horseback borrowed and returned to his father's property. Arthur told officers he dropped the equipment at the barn. It was evident he had not because the hounds detected the scent to the home's kitchen door. He was lying. Sherriff Collins was also aware of the resentment between stepson and stepmother, and she ordered Arthur's arrest, direct evidence or not, for murder. When a deputy sheriff apprehended the man, he noted Inez Palmer ran from the home and, most inappropriately, kissed Arthur quite passionately on the lips.

Maude Collins was probably under a considerable amount of pressure to solve the crime under the circumstances that she was the first woman to hold the sheriff's job in Ohio. She had not been handed the position.

Sheriff Maude Collins was bright, observative, and articulate. On February 17th, 1927, a Grand Jury indicted Arthur for the crime. On March 10th, Collins received a call from the Oreton Post Office, where folks from Axtel Ridge received their mail, stating Inez Palmer had left a message for her. The woman revealed that Bill Stout had suddenly left to go out West and start a new life. He would never return.

Sheriff Collins was immediately suspicious. After Sarah's death, Bill Stout had moved into his son's home on the ridge along an old dirt road with Inez and his grandsons. His grandsons needed family close by, and the widowed farmer needed someone to cook and care for him. All along, Bill Stout refused to believe his son had murdered his wife. "I can't believe that Arthur did it," he had said adamantly. "But if he did, he certainly ought to be punished. If he is indicted and tried, then I'll want to tell the jury that he was a good boy, but I'll have to admit he and Sarah didn't get along—" That Bill would suddenly decide to leave his home in Vinton County and his close family seemed absurd. But had Bill been the killer after all and left town as not to be arrested?

Old road along Axtel Ridge Sheriff Collins would have used.

Sheriff Collins immediately took the old dirt and rutted road to remote Axtel Ridge. She questioned Inez Palmer at Arthur Stout's home to investigate this new twist in the homicide case. However, when police arrived at the scene and discovered Bill had left his car and belongings, it was clear there was foul play. Upon Inez Palmer's directions, Collins followed a set of large-boot footprints to a field Bill had allegedly taken to mend a fence the day he left. She discovered a lunch pail along the route, and within, a makeshift will bequeathing both farms to Arthur Stout alone. Even more suspect, Collins observed the boot prints were not embedded deeply enough in the soft earth for a man's heavy weight. Upon returning, the sheriff saw the boys, Artie and William, lugging buckets of water from the creek; she questioned the two why they were not taking water from a perfectly good well behind the house. One answered that Inez had told them not to take water from the well; it was not fit to drink anymore. The sheriff rushed to the well, peered downward, and found Bill Stout's corpse dumped in the water partway down.

The well, right, where the body was dumped.

Pieces of a ghastly puzzle would fall into place when, not long after, Artie and William confessed their father had encouraged and talked often at the dinner table about murdering his parents, eventually persuading Inez and the children to do the dirty deed. It was a cold-blooded and well-calculated plan laid out after he offered Inez's brother $50.00 to commit the murders, and the young man had refused.

Artie would admit that one morning Inez had talked him into going to the home of the elder Stouts. She made it appear her visit was nothing more than a quick, benign chat and "—by the way, while we are here, could Arthur borrow Bill's gun?" Sarah had nodded. Was she walking into some trap? Indeed, she was suspicious of the motive. Was Inez toying with her fears she would be murdered right there? Certainly not with little Artie by her side! Sarah had taken the bait, even if reluctantly. Her head was probably swimming with doubt, fear gripping her soul. Together, the three entered the home. As Sarah stooped over in the closet to get the weapon, Inez swooped forward and hit the old woman over the head with a weight. She then leaped on her back and choked her to death with a strip of a bedsheet. Next, Inez demanded the boy pour kerosene on the body and light it on fire to hide the evidence. But the linoleum would not catch fire as they planned; instead, the small flames barely singed the woman's dead body, clothing, and hair.

As for Bill's death in Arthur Stout's home, Inez bided her time, waiting for him to sit by the fireplace one chilly March night in 1927, just as he always did. A neighbor once remarked that most evenings, Inez would play on a little piano in the home, pounding the keys incessantly and singing off-key at the top of her lungs until Bill moved in with the youngsters. Once there, he made her stop, telling Inez that it was disrespectable to his dead wife's memory.

Inez had watched the old man lean forward to poke the fire, then beat him in the back of the head with a piece of cordwood. She, Artie, and William dragged the cumbersome load to the well and shoved the old man into its dark depths. Inez had attempted to cover up Bill's murder by donning a pair of his boots and walking to the field to make it appear he had been mending fences. She had faked the will. The night Bill disappeared, the sound of fingers banging the keys of a piano and the caterwauling voice of the young woman swept again through the hills. It crept along the misty hollows, above a creek, and then up another hill to a neighbor's ears whose home overlooked Arthur Stout's house. Those who heard had known something was amiss.

And one of probably 20 of my orange fear-flags.

Another old road fading away along Axtel Ridge.

One late afternoon, I followed the old roads and paths to the remains of the house where Arthur and Inez lived before sent to prison for the murders of Sarah and Bill Stout. I pushed aside the thick brush, zig-zagging through the pine trees tying orange vinyl tape to limbs and looking back each time anxiously to make sure the thin trail was well-marked.

The ruins of the old house.

I suspected no foul play as I wandered around the area of the old house and finally stood where Inez Palmer murdered Bill Stout and dumped his body into the well. I found pieces of old dishes, a broken beer bottle, and an old cooking pot. I waited for a ghost, but none showed. Although it has been passed on to me from families who lived in and near Oreton years ago that the house and land where I stood was haunted, I was unsure if it was Bill Stout, his murderous son, or even his son's young lover Inez who was once said to make an appearance.

It was getting dark, too dark for my lonesome self to trace back my steps with only the help of orange vinyl streamers clinging desperately to trees now fading in a misty fog and a persnickety cell phone to guide my way. The rain that had been holding off was starting to become steady in the evening gloom. I was a bit disappointed, but I know the dead do not rise for anyone but themself.

My shadow makes an eerie addition to the site where the well (in the middle of the picture) used to be. It has long been passed down that groans issued from within and strange things happened near it. I did not hear anything. Thank God. It would be a long sprint back to my jeep.

I sighed. I had an hour or so to traverse the eerie and seemingly endless miles of pine trees to return to the safety of my jeep. Good grief, I certainly did not want to get lost! Far off, there was a hunter camp. Once in a while, in the nearly silent air, I could hear the gentle flow of a radio playing and hear a truck chug down a gravel road.

I started to retrace my steps. I came upon one vinyl orange streamer, plucked it from the dead branch I tied it on, and searched for the next. Easy-peasy. I found another barely clinging to the limb. With some difficulty, I had to struggle to find the third and fourth because they were lying on the ground. I was confident I tied those knots tight. Perhaps not, though. I sighed and noted that for next time, I would be more cautious.

Yet, the path seemed slightly different, as if I was going right, then left along the ridge. I was sure my original trail was straight. I did not think the streamers would have blown that far away. Instead, I was zig-zagging right to left and closer to the edge of the crest than I remember. I had hiked straight down the center. I heard the music, still far off, and the sound of it should have been comforting. It was not. It was behind me and not in front. Was that the sound of fingers banging a piano? Or my imagination?

I wandered aimlessly but managed to see a bit of what I believed was an old dirt path covered in autumn leaves and pine needles beneath my feet. I swear, for a moment, I was a mile off my original route. My heart was pounding. I kept forging forward, getting that awful anxiety gripping my chest as I found two more of my streamers lying on the pine needle forest floor. What the heck? Perhaps it was the wind untying my loose knots and tossing them to the breeze. Or perhaps not. The pine trees around me were starting to swirl. Surely nobody else was out here toying with me, thinking it was funny to move my tiny trail banners. I waited for laughter. There was none. Then I saw it, up ahead—a small streamer clinging to a pine tree near my main path that would take me to the old dirt road. I sighed in relief and set my sights right on it—until I stopped dead in my tracks.

As I stood there and right before my eyes, the little strand of orange vinyl tape I had so carefully tied on that specific branch unraveled all on its own, wiggle-wiggle like unseen fingers were unwinding the ends. It clung to the knotted limb, untangled and rippling, not three seconds before a bit of wind took it to the ground and off into the darkness. I shuddered. Was this a game, well calculated, scheming? I felt dizzy again, but only because I was holding my breath.

I made hasty steps to my jeep. I did not want to be stuck on Axtel Ridge alone in the darkness with things that were manipulating, coldblooded, and toying with my greatest fear reflected in my nightmares that something sniffed out and identified deep within me. Just like they had done to Sarah. Just like they had done to Bill. Because I knew it was not only one calculating being there this night unraveling my orange vinyl streamers one by one and letting each ride the wind. It was two. And they knew exactly what they were doing. Because now they are not alone on the ridge anymore. They are with me every night, lurking only steps behind me when I get lost in my nightmares.

Little remains of the old house on the hill as nature takes over except my hiking buddy Lucy who always seems to find a way to get into the pictures for a pose. I do not mind. She is the only one who does not complain when I search for haunted places, hiking for miles and miles and for hours at a time. When I say, "Okay, let's go another twenty minutes or so. I know it is just around the bend." She never pouts and grumbles that I said that the last six times.

Timmons (Ray) Covered Bridge
(No longer there!)
Old OH-327
Ray, Ohio 45672

The Legend of Enos Kay

The Timmons Covered Bridge before it was razed circa mid-1930s. Photo courtesy Nyla Timmons Holdren and the Vinton County Historical & Genealogical Society.

Many years ago, between Ray and Chillicothe and over the Middle Fork of Salt Creek, a covered bridge ran through the Timmons Property. A ghost resided there that would frighten young couples either passing through or stopping to steal a kiss within its dark corridor.

One time, as a young woman and man were about halfway through the bridge in their covered buggy, the top came crashing down on them with a hard snap! Above, a man's hazy face appeared and drifted down toward them. The horse bolted, and the carriage tipped, dumping the couple in the dark while it disappeared down the dirt road. Many couples had to walk home in the darkness, and their trysts were spoiled by the ghost. After a while, courting couples avoided that bridge on the road altogether.

The Timmons Covered Bridge. Photo courtesy Nyla Timmons Holdren and the Vinton County Historical & Genealogical Society.

The ghost's existence has been explained like this— sometime in the early years of the bridge, a young man named Enos Kay committed suicide there. A handsome and popular boy, he had grown up in the fertile farmlands and towns near Hamden and Ray. He was only in his teens when he fell hard in love with a pretty local girl named Alvira. She loved him dearly too. He would scrimp and save over the next two years, preparing for their wedding. The sweethearts would often sneak away to be alone, meeting at the Timmons Covered Bridge away from prying eyes.

But just a week before the couple would wed, the preacher at a local church offered a picnic. All the young people in the community excitedly attended as it was the perfect place to meet new friends or find a sweetheart amongst the crowd. One of the young men present was a newcomer to the area, a Mister Brown who was quite handsome, strapping, and charming. He swept all the girls off their feet, including Alvira, as he shared a piece of apple pie with her. In just one warm afternoon, Enos was hardly a memory in the back of Alvira's mind. Two nights would pass. Alvira's new suitor shoved a ladder beneath her bedroom window, and the two eloped.

Over the following days, Alvira and Mister Brown's exciting and romantic flight was all the neighbors would talk about even when Enos Kay could hear. He was heartbroken and angry, and only a week would pass when Enos Kay threw a fist into the air and vowed: "I'll kill myself and haunt fool lovers 'til the judgment day!"

Where the Timmons Covered Bridge once stood.

Enos hanged himself from the very bridge rafters where he had met with Alvira. Only two days after he made the oath and died, the ghostly appearances at the Timmons Covered Bridge began. They would still be going on there if the bridge was not destroyed many years ago as a newer state route was built nearby to handle the increasing traffic from Chillicothe to Athens. Only the creek and a few foundation stones remain on private property.

Nyla Timmons Holdren, below, who grew up near the old covered bridge recalled a story her grandmother, Suzie Baker Timmons, once told to her. As a young woman Suzie Timmons was riding through the covered bridge at night when a dark shadowy figure grabbed a hold of the horse's bridle that was pulling her carriage. So startled was Miss Timmons that she gave a quick snap of her whip and the horse quickened his steps and got the carriage through. She never knew what had tried to seize the horse, but recounted the story to her children and grandchildren through the years.

Both the Timmons Covered Bridge and the old road where it once stood is long gone. The road is defunct and now runs into private property. The bridge was not used after 1953. However, do not worry. You only have to drive a few miles west for a ghostly treat. If you are looking for a scare, the legend advises that Enos Kay will find any lovers who park in remote areas nearby and haunt them!

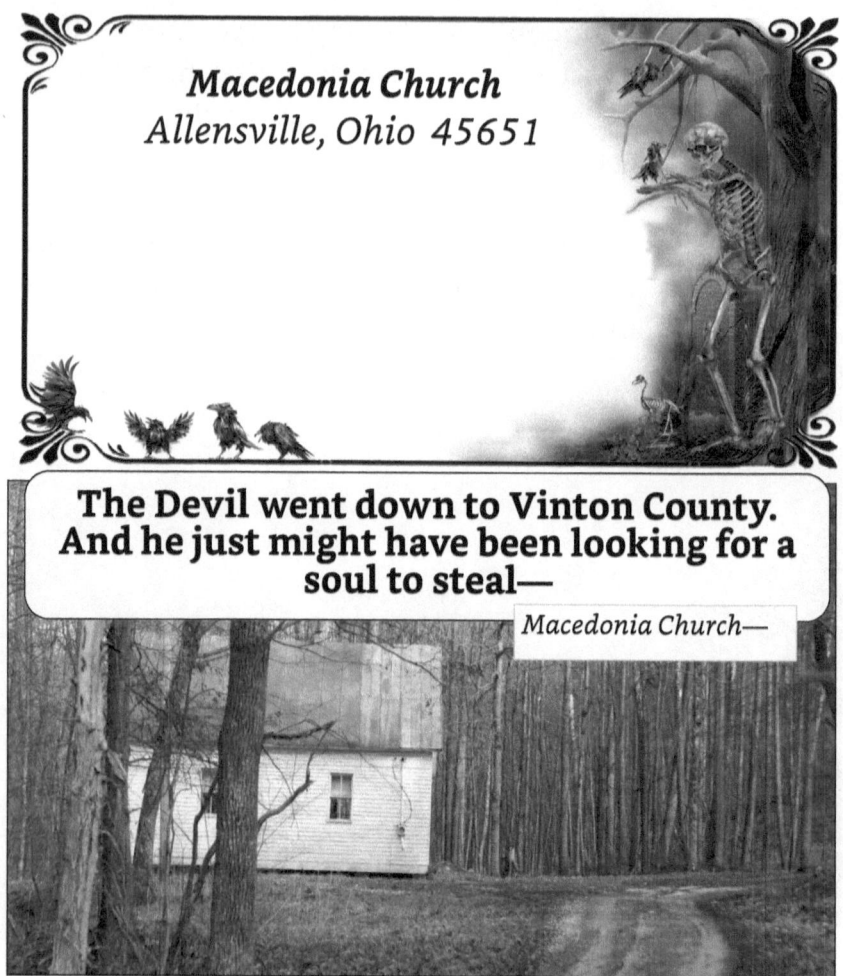

Macedonia Church
Allensville, Ohio 45651

The Devil went down to Vinton County. And he just might have been looking for a soul to steal—

Macedonia Church—

A reporter from the Hocking Sentinel claimed that Satan, himself, showed up at the Macedonia Church Revival one cold February evening of 1886—

If we are to credit a correspondent of the Adelphi Border News, the pious people of Salt Creek township are troubled with a veritable ghost, hob-goblin or devil, as you please. That paper states: "During service at Macedonia church, in their recent revival, the devil appeared in person before the alter, and when spoke to would not answer or leave till prayer was offered. He was a giant in size and had hands with claws like an eagle, and head and horns like a Texas steer, and as black as coal." Hocking Sentinel., February 11, 1886. Local Items.

Macedonia Church tucked into the woods. If the devil assumed the humble souls of this tiny church were easy prey, he greatly underestimated the spirit of the people of the county. Had he known better, he would never have come between those folks and their gospel.

The alter where the devil and the church folks made their stand.

Lake Rupert
OH-683
Hamden, Ohio 45634
39.202809, -82.536873

Great Ball of Fire

The area of the ball of fire—

Before the city of Wellston dammed the Little Raccoon Creek making Lake Rupert, travelers who took a little lane off Hamden-Allensville Road heard ghostly footsteps when passing an old wooden bridge over the creek. If it was near midnight and there were those among them brave enough to follow, they would see a ball of fire drifting above a grave where it stopped.

Beard Cemetery
Sam Russell Road
Hamden, Ohio 45634
39.194855, -82.429154

Black Dog

Beard Cemetery and the road where the Black Dog is seen—

On a lone dirt-gravel road often unpassable during heavy rain or snows, there is a lonely cemetery. Although it once had a schoolhouse nearby, little remains of its past except for old trees and headstones. Those who have traveled to the little graveyard have seen a black dog keeping pace with their vehicle. But as they pull into the little lot by the cemetery gate, it vanishes. Some have seen a Civil War soldier standing at attention near a grave. When he disappears, the grave glows green.

The Ghost Towns & Their Ghosts

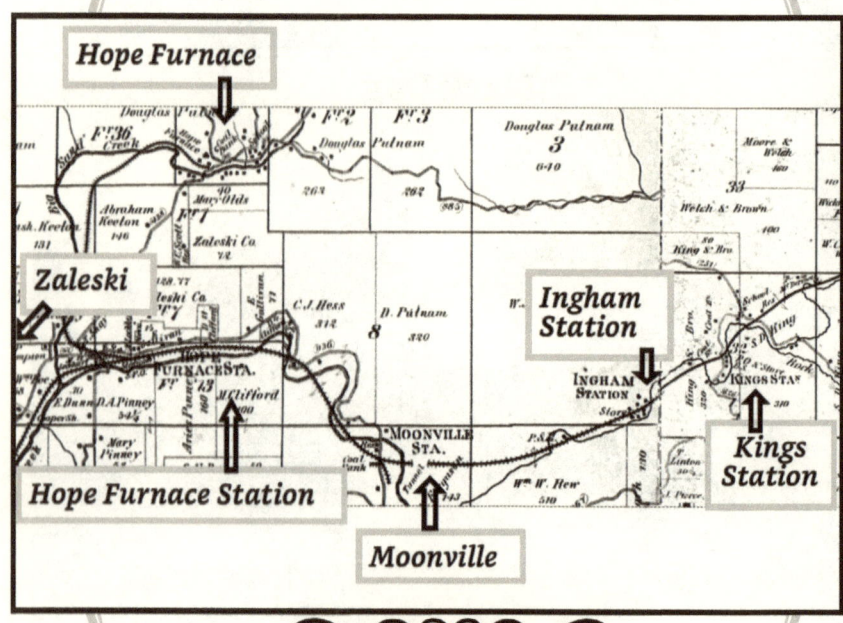

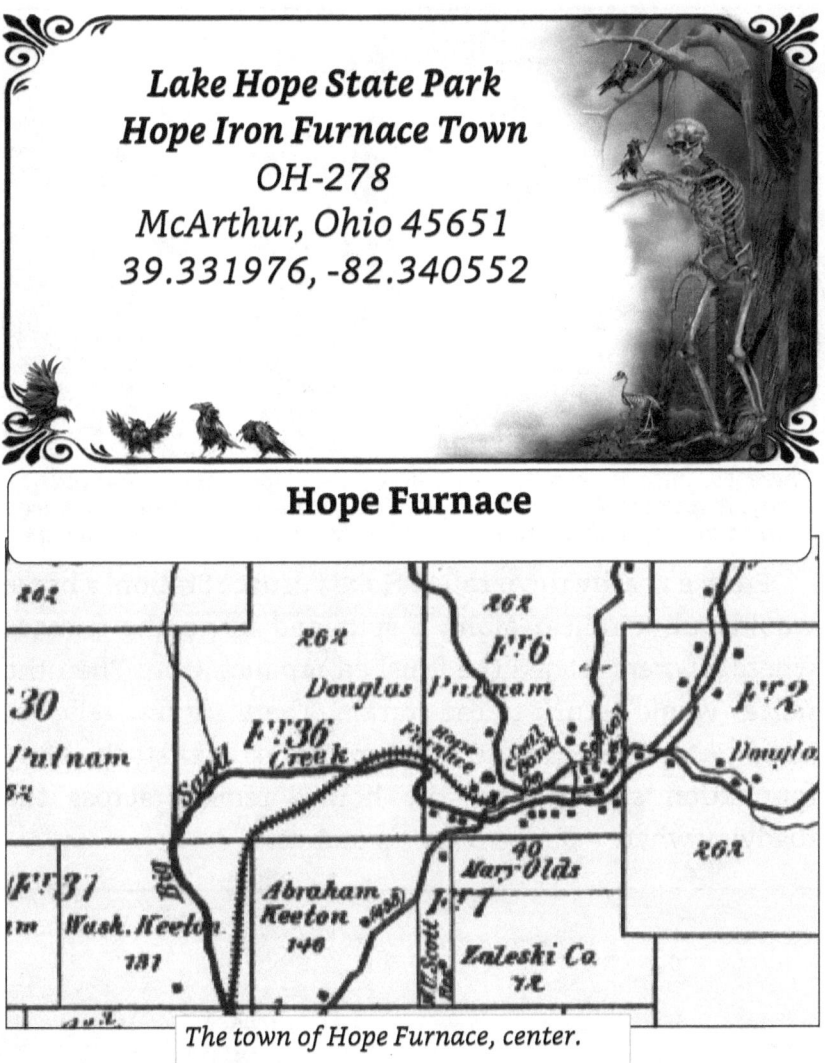

Lake Hope State Park
Hope Iron Furnace Town
OH-278
McArthur, Ohio 45651
39.331976, -82.340552

Hope Furnace

The town of Hope Furnace, center.

Hope Furnace was one of 69 charcoal iron furnaces in the Hanging Rock Region, open from 1854 to 1874 and initially run by the Big Sand Iron Company. Fueling and running the furnace required hundreds of laborers who worked at the furnace, cut timber, or drove oxen teams to haul the ore. The charcoal (made by the stacking, then burning cut wood) used to fuel the furnace was produced in the surrounding forest, then hauled by oxen.

The furnace.

There was once an iron furnace where Lake Hope State Park stands today. A spur track of railroad led to the furnace from Hope Furnace Station so the finished product could be transported by railroad cars.

From a nearby town called Hope Furnace Station, a horse would pull a railcar along a spur and up to the furnace where laborers loaded the finished product, iron. Then the railcar would return to the station. There are few relics of Hope Furnace's past left except its stone stack. Only foundation stones from the homes remain across the roadway where a pine grove now stands.

The furnace.

Where much of the town of Hope Furnace once stood is now a forest along Olds Hollow Trail. However, the keen eye can pick out old foundation stones and bricks beneath the leaves and pine needles.

Many workers and families lived across the road from the furnace in cabins or commuted from other close towns. Other folks lived around the furnace like the Olds family, the Sheas, and Abraham Keeton, who owned a farm with sheep, hogs, and cattle. It is difficult to believe there was once a general store and outbuildings, a one-room schoolhouse, and small cabins for workers and families. The stack from the iron furnace and an old cemetery are pretty much all remaining to remind us that a rather large company town existed there. Well, unless you believe in ghosts. But, then, that is another story—

Night Watchman

Above the stack, center, where the ill-fated worker has been seen carrying a lantern. State Route 278 is to the rear of the image.

Sometime during the twenty years that the furnace made the iron, a night watchman overlooking the furnace fell to his death into the furnace's fiery pit. Almost immediately after, when the bosses would have their meetings in one building on the property, there would be several loud bangs upon the door. When answered, nobody was there. Workers would also often see the dead man's lantern bobbing within the building. Later, when the buildings were gone, travelers along the roadway would see the glow of a lantern light floating above the old stack.

Burnt Cabin

The town of Hope Furnace as seen today begins here. Homes were scattered along Route 278 mainly across from the iron furnace ruins, but met up with the small town of Zaleski.

After the end of the Civil War, two brothers working for the Hope Iron Furnace company as coalers lived in a small wooden shack across from the furnace. One night, the building burned to the ground, and the two died within. No one thought it could be foul play as both young men were well-liked. It was mid-November and chilly. Most assumed one or the other had started a fire to warm the thin-walled building by pouring into a tin bucket filled with wood, some lantern oil made of camphene, a dangerous but cheap mixture of turpentine, alcohol, and camphor oil. And it exploded. Not long after, those passing the area of the burnt building heard angry shouting issuing from the charred remains, but after a thorough search of the site, the curious found no source for the commotion.

Five years would pass, and in Tennessee, police arrested a man named John Slavens for killing his nephew. He was tried and found guilty. As authorities were preparing to take him to prison, his wife confessed that she knew of two others the man had murdered. It was two young brothers who worked at a furnace in Ohio. Her husband had robbed them of their pay, murdered them, then burned their cabin to the ground to hide his crimes. It was the two young men who lived at Hope Furnace. Upon hearing of the double murder, vigilantes broke down the prison doors and dragged Slavens to a tree. They tied a noose around his neck and hanged him.

Many years have passed, and nothing remains of the little burnt cabin in the woods but a few old foundation stones piled along with others. The charred remnants of its walls have long decayed, a pine forest with a blanket of needles lays atop, and anybody who knew the men have been dead and buried for a long time. Occasionally, hikers taking the Olds Hollow Trail above Sandy Run and across from the ruins of the furnace have heard strange shouts and moans among the pines. They nosy around, searching for clues for the unrest. But nothing is found.

Pioneer Cemetery Lights

The old Pioneer Cemetery for Hope Furnace.

If you are standing at the furnace, you can look across State Route 278 and into the thick forest of pines where part of the company town was located. There is a trail there, dark and somber, called Olds Hollow Trail. If you follow it beneath the shades of pine boughs, it will lead you along the old paths of the company town and to the Hope Furnace Pioneer Cemetery. The cemetery was established in 1853 and used until 1865. There were nearly 60 residents buried here, like five-year-old Sarah Burns and 59-year-old John Gibson. Now few stones remain. But some have seen tiny lights flickering at the cemetery and along the hills where more dead are buried in unmarked graves.

Hope Furnace Station
Along Moonville Rail Trail
Wheelabout Road
McArthur, Ohio 45651
39.317339, -82.351269
to
39.315995, -82.332643

The Desperate Twinkling

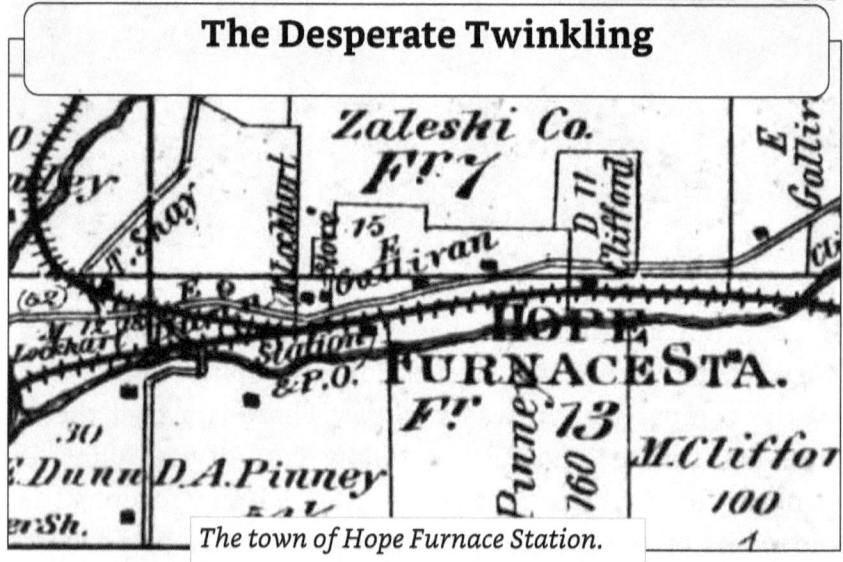

The town of Hope Furnace Station.

Hope Furnace Station, a mile and a half away from Hope Furnace, was a coal mining, iron transport, and lumbering village along the railway. People walking the tracks through town would see twinkling lights following them along the path—tiny orbs gleaming bright to faint over and over as if someone with two small lanterns was trying desperately to get their attention. Locals explained the lights as this: In the 1860s, a devoted family man and perfectionist tidied up his finances, completed all his business affairs, and gave his son a box with all the family's valuable papers.

He purchased powder and lead, loaded a musket, walked to the tracks, and shot himself. When the twinkling lights began, some believed that the man who had been so thorough in life forgot to do something before his death. He was trying to tell those passing what he had neglected. But no one was ever able to figure out what he was trying to divulge to them.

To access the Rail Trail through Hope Furnace Station where the ghostly lights were seen—

Parking at Hope Furnace Station Schoolhouse:
27961-28157 Wheelabout Road
McArthur, Ohio 45651
39.315947, -82.352071
Park at the schoolhouse and follow the backpacking trail signs by the kiosk to Hope-Moonville Road. You will pass the Rail Trail on the right just after crossing the bridge on the road.

Rail Trail Start Point along Wheelabout Road:
39.317339, -82.351269
Hiking to Hope-Moonville Road
39.315995, -82.332643
Along the one-mile, one-way rail trail path, you will pass the area where travelers have witnessed the mysterious lights.

Between Hope Furnace Station and Moonville
Site of Train Wreck
Rail Trail by Hope-Moonville Road
McArthur, Ohio 45651
39.312348, -82.329167

No Man's Land

Site of Red Landrum wreck.

On the Monday of December 26th of 1938, the 63-car Baltimore and Ohio freight train was careening eastward-bound down the lonely line of railroad tracks in a driving, icy rain between Moonville and Hope Furnace Station, about 6 miles east of Zaleski.

It was a deserted run of railway, a seemingly God-forsaken mile after mile of nothing but thick, dark forest—a virtual no man's land. There were few people now living along the abandoned route from the tiny village of Mineral to the quiet town of Zaleski; the booming coal and iron days were long gone. The wilderness had gobbled up any signs of civilization between the communities. Most townspeople had deserted their homes, the building's skeletal remains enduring now as bent and decaying wooden frames barely able to keep their stand against the winter winds. All that remained were a handful of abandoned cemeteries to leave evidence a few souls had once even lived there.

It was a chilly winter night. The hint of an icy gale to come the next day was already forcing the temperature to spiral downward. Impending winds as high as 35 miles per hour were heading towards McArthur, Allensville, and Athens. 54-year-old Charles "Red" Landrum, a veteran of the railroad and father of three, who hailed originally from Jackson and then Chillicothe, was engineering the ill-fated train. He was on the lead engine of the double-header freight No. 88. He had no clue as the train sped around a bend that there had been a rockslide with a 100-ton boulder resting along the tracks until he caught it in his headlights too late. The train plowed full-speed straight into the enormous pile of rocks nearly 21 feet high. The train and its second engine were derailed along with 12 of the 63 cars. The ensuing collision pinned Engineer Landrum in the cab with a broken leg, and he was scalded to death by the steam.

By December 28th, crews of 200 men had cleared the track of the wreckage, derailed cars, and stone. They did not, however, clear the path of everything. The ghost of Engineer Landrum still haunts the railway in that no man's land between Hope Furnace Station and old Moonville.

Wreck Area along one of the bleakest sections of the B & O between Hope Furnace Station and Moonville. Courtesy of the Estate of John R. Grabb. His book: *The Marietta & Cincinnati railroad and its successor, the Baltimore & Ohio: a study of this once great route across Ohio, 1851-1988* hosts many images of trains in the region and is available for purchase.

When the weather suddenly starts to hint of a storm on chilly December nights, hikers have seen a contorted shadow shuffling in the cut in the hill where the wreck occurred. Some hear the piercing cry of that doomed, long-gone train's wheels on the tracks, the wail of its horn, and a deep, mournful moan before it fades away to nothing.

The cut in the hill (as seen now) where Charles "Red" Landrum's train collided with a fall of rock.

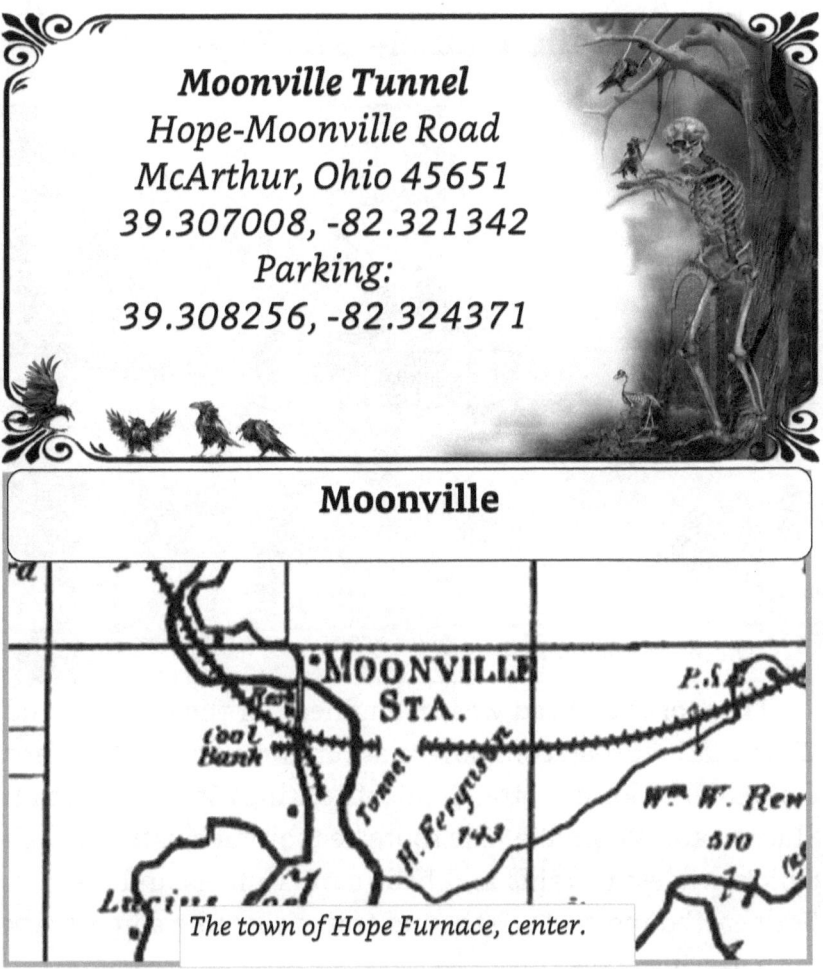

Moonville Tunnel
Hope-Moonville Road
McArthur, Ohio 45651
39.307008, -82.321342
Parking:
39.308256, -82.324371

Moonville

The town of Hope Furnace, center.

Moonville proper was a tiny village of a couple of families—the Fergusons and the Coes. However, many families lived in the outlying region and used the railroad pathway through Moonville to get from one town to another. It had a post office called Rew, a schoolhouse, a cemetery, a depot, a mine, and a grist mill and sawmill. Even when the railway ran through the area, and the coal mines thrived, the route through Moonville was dreaded by engineers because it was such an isolated community. This remoteness and the unusually large number of deaths on the railroad around a tunnel in Moonville led to many ghost stories and legends.

Moonville Tunnel—The Engineer

The Moonville Tunnel—

Theodore Lawhead was an engineer for the Marietta and Cincinnati railroad company that ran through southeastern Ohio towns like Marietta, Chillicothe, Kings Station, Ingham Station, and Moonville. The route he took cut a path through Ohio's wildest terrains and had many tunnels and trestles. Both eastbound and westbound trains shared a single track with passing areas.

One November night in 1880, while Lawhead was heading through southern Ohio, the dispatch failed to notify the eastbound train of the westbound's route and time. The two collided near Moonville Tunnel, and Lawhead and his fireman died instantly. After the wreck, many of the trainmen feared going along that stretch of the railroad. They said they would see the flicker of lantern light when they came along a certain section of the tracks near the tunnel in Moonville. As they got closer, a robed figure would join the flicker of lantern light and step out toward the train before vanishing.

Frank Lawhead, Engineer Killed in Train Wreck Near Kings station in this county on Thursday last, Engineer Lawhead and Charles Krick, fireman, both of Chillicothe, were instantly killed by collision of freight trains, which, we are told, was the result of a mistake of train dispatcher. The trains were totally wrecked. **Athens Messenger, 11/11/1880**

Since then, there have been countless eyewitnesses claiming they have seen odd lights flitting about the tunnel akin to a lantern swinging back and forth. There have been photo images of a foggy mist and even a few who have taken pictures of an apparition of a man in an engineer hat walking at the far end. The sound of a train has been heard and the creaking of a gate echoes somewhere—and yet no trains have come through the area in more than 30 years!

The ghost of Moonville, after an absence of one year, has returned and is again at its old pranks, haunting B&O S-W freight trains and their crews. Monday night the ghost appeared just east of the cut, which is one half mile the other side of Moonville. It showed up in front of fast freight No. 99 west bound, which is due at Moonville at 8:50 p.m. The train was hauled by engine 226, in charge of Engineer William Washburn. The conductor was Mr. Charles Bazler. The ghost was attired in a pure white robe, and carried a lantern. It had a flowing white beard, its eyes glistened like balls of fire, and surrounding it was a halo of twinkling stars. As the train approached, the lantern was swung across the track. Engineer Washburn gave the proper whistle signal, and stopped the train. As he did so, his ghostship stepped off the track and disappeared amidst the rocks near by. This is not the first time the same ghost has stopped and delayed the trains. It has been at that business, off and on, since the frightful collision at that point, in which Engineer Lawhead lost his life and Engineer Wash Walters was injured. **Chillicothe Gazette—1/23/1895.**

Moonville Tunnel—The Brakeman

Brakemen for the railroad were usually younger men between the ages of 16 and 25. They were required to walk atop a railcar and manually apply the brakes to the moving train, which was an especially dangerous task on southeastern Ohio's twists, turns, uphills, and downhills.

There were at least four brakemen killed on the railway near Moonville Tunnel. Witnesses report they have seen a man carrying a lantern limping along the tracks and through the tunnel, only to disappear just as he eases into a dark spot within the darkness—

Locals tell the story like this:

Many years ago, a young brakeman collected his pay. He had worked hard all week and decided that his hard labor was worthy of a good, hard drink in town. So on his way home, he stopped in at a tavern in Zaleski. But one drink led to another until he was so drunk, he could barely walk.

Sometime after dark, he left the bar with a bottle in hand and began to walk the tracks toward home. Partway, he determined he was due a nap and laid down on the stones still warm from the day's sun and rested his head on a rise. As he fell fast to sleep, the bottle slipped from his fingers.

But unfortunately, he did not contemplate that the rocks for his bed were the ballast from the train track, and his pillow was a rail, and during the night, a train passed through.

The next day, a miner walking the tracks spotted the bottle lying near a railroad tie and reached down to pick it up. There were droplets of blood not far away. He heard a low moaning, "That's mine." Looking around, the startled man saw nobody nearby but followed the bloody trail to the brush near the tracks. He found the young man's dead body, mashed by the train.

After, locals would recall seeing the young brakeman staggering along the tracks just after the tunnel and before the first trestle. He would pause, waver there a moment before crumpling into a heap on the railroad ties. But before he fell, he would drop something peculiar to the ground. Then he would disappear altogether. Some were curious enough to search out the ghost and try to determine what had fallen from his fingers. When they investigated the place the item had dropped, a voice would seep from the brush, "That's mine."

Moonville Tunnel—The Bully

David "Baldie" Keeton was a farmer who lived near Hope Furnace Station and Moonville for a long, long time. He was 65 years old in 1886 and still as big and stalwart as he had been when he was a young man. Everybody knew Baldie's temperamental nature. He was a bully who beat his wife and picked on anyone smaller than his size.

When he went to the local bar, he liked to pick out the littlest man in the room and give him a bear hug so hard that the other man could not breathe, and eventually, it would knock him out. Nobody wanted to be around Baldie, and certainly, nobody wanted to make him cross.

One evening, after returning from a court appearance in Zaleski, Baldie stopped off at the bar. He got drunk then got into a barroom brawl. He lost the fight, and the owner of the bar told him to leave town or else. He did leave, but Baldie did not make it far. When he did not return home, his wife assumed that he had gotten drunk and slept it off with nearby family.

When he did not contact anyone for a couple of days, she sent out a party to search for him. Instead, they found his mangled corpse on the tracks. Most everyone from Hope Furnace to Mineral believed he was dead long before the first, second, and third train hit him, and they were glad for it even if they did not say it aloud.

Mothers in the vicinity would warn their children not to go near the tracks and not stay out after dark. If they did, old Baldie Keeton might get them. It seems that his ghost was often seen hunched over and shuffling drunkenly along the railroad between Zaleski and Moonville Tunnel, grumbling to himself. He is also spotted above the tunnel, standing still and solitary and known to throw rocks and pebbles at those walking beneath. ***Here is how the locals talked about Baldie:***

It seems that Keeton, who was forty-eight years old at the time and was a Moonville resident, decided to go to the Hope-Moonville saloon (probably Lockhart's). He became exceedingly drunk and got into a bar room brawl. He evidently lost the fight and was told to leave town or else. I guess he was a little slow in leaving and was bushwhacked and killed on his way home. The next morning he was found with no money and the coroner diagnosed it as murder. His killers were never found. There is a David Keeton buried in the Keeton Cemetery, and if it's the same one, then this story took place in 1886—**As told by John Wyman, From Historical Archives at Alice's House – Vinton County Historical Society**

Baldie Keeton (David) was big and powerful and when in a fight or fallin' around he would hug a man and squeeze him. One day in Mat Lockhart's saloon he tried to squeeze Jim Mace and Jim knocked him over the bar and into the bottles. Then he got Baldie's head and bent his over the bar ready to break his neck but was talked out of it. A Dunn tried to break it up earlier in the fight and Jim "damn near killed him". Baldie was finally killed near the coal washer near the Bighouse place-supposedly by a train but everyone figured he was murdered. **Frank Mace, October 17, 1961**

Moonville Tunnel—Lavender Lady

For years, those visiting Moonville have seen a ghostly woman float across the bridge closest to the Moonville Tunnel parking lot, along the old railroad bed, then through the tunnel. When she nears the far end of the tunnel, she makes a jagged turn and vanishes. Those who do not see her and who are in her path have caught the faint scent of lavender perfume. Most think little of the scent and decided it must be the smell of flowers wafting up from the valley below. However, there are others who know of the ghosts of Moonville and the flowery scent makes them shudder. Here is the reason for their unease—

There was an old woman who lived in a little house not far from Moonville. One day, while she was walking the tracks, she was hit on the trestle and dragged clear to Moonville Tunnel before the train could come to a stop. After, her ghost would walk from the train trestle through the tunnel and disappear on the other side. But not without a warning she was coming.

In the 1800s, perfumes were not usually applied directly to the skin as they are today. Instead, women blotted rose, lemon, or lavender botanicals on kerchiefs or clothing, unless they were using the oils as a rubbing salve to remedy aches and pains. Some believe that lavender was the particular oil the old woman had used as a perfume or massaged on her aching elbows or knees that fateful day prior to taking her last journey. Because before her ghost would pass by, startled bystanders would catch the heavy scent of lavender wafting in the air. And some still do!

Ingham Station—Lost Hand

You can find the area of Ingham Station and Bear Hollow while walking the rail trail from Moonville to King Station. Look for the second and larger body of water about a mile from the tunnel.

The lonely stretch of dark railway continued past Moonville Tunnel. About a mile away was the coal mining town of Ingham Station, founded by brothers W. J. & J.M. Ingham. Little more than foundations, a well, and old mines are left to show the village with a grocery store, railway station, school, and houses even existed at all. The mines employed 10 - 14 employees, and a dozen or so lived in the town. Now there is just a ghost—a coal miner who hitched a ride on a train in 1907.

The last time anybody saw middle-aged coalminer Allan Albaugh was Saturday, August 24th, 1907. He had been drinking when he hopped on a train at Zaleski with a jug of whiskey in his hand. He was heading for his home in Luhrig near Athens. For several days, nobody heard from him, so a search party was sent out to find him. Soon enough, they discovered his hand near Moonville Tunnel.

While walking the tracks at Bear Hollow near Ingham Station, Frank McWhorter smelled something dead and found the rest of Albaugh rotted and covered in maggots. Later, some who walked the railroad from Moonville to Ingham Station said they saw a one-handed man walking the tracks with eyes peeled to the ground. It was Albaugh's ghost searching for his hand.

Local resident, Mike Shea, related the discovery of Albaugh's body in this way to historian/naturalist Bill Price—*Allan Albaugh was drinking and hopped a train at Zaleski with a jug of whiskey. No one heard from him. They found him dead this side of Ingham near Bear Hollow. Mike Shea smelled him one day and Frank McWhorter and a one-eyed fellow found him when attracted by the smell. He was full of maggots, been dead several days.* **Mike Shea, 1961**

Just Outside the County Line

Just over the Athens County Line—
Kings Station Stalker

Kings Switch was a mining town located just across the Athens County line and founded by Silas D. King. Mister King donated some of his lands for a train station, and the town thrived. It had 40 coalminers , a general store, rows of houses, a school, and a post office during its heyday. But like most of the coal towns seen along the Rail Trail, its life faded away as the coal mining industry in the region subsided. Little remains of the old town but a few buildings. And there is a tunnel and a ghost story—

A couple of miles east along the old railroad from Moonville is the town of Kings Station, and just another mile more is Mineral. The railway and coal mining were not the only things linking these three towns together. They had a ghost. It was common to walk the railway from one of these towns to the next, whether for work or groceries or visiting family and friends. The tracks were the shortest route, and they also were the least likely to be flooded as the railway built them on higher ground.

One night during a long week of rain and when the valleys had flooded, a young man set off on the tracks from Mineral toward Moonville to meet his father. When he made it to Kings Station and its tunnel, he noticed a woman in a white dress walking just ahead of him. The faster he walked, the faster she walked. She kept pace for quite some time before suddenly, she disappeared. He knew at some point if he continued, he might have to pass her. Frightened, the young man ran with eyes glued to the tracks without stopping until he made it to Moonville. The ghost was later identified as a woman named Sarah Hewitt who had, just weeks after giving birth in June 1878, committed suicide by slitting her own throat with a razor. She had been married less than a year and lived a couple of miles from Mineral.

Here is how one townsperson heard the story—

"There was a man by the name of Earnest Keeton that lived in the neighborhood. Earnest had the tendency to tip the bottle a little on occasion. Back at that time there was no road that led from Hope to Mineral. People walked the railroad back and forth, and he had been somewhere over in the vicinity of Mineral, possibly the church or whatever. But he was coming back by himself, and as he was walking along on one end of the ties he noticed on the opposite end of the ties there was a figure that was following right along beside of him at the same speed that he was traveling. He started to speed up a little bit and it speeded up a little bit and watched it and noticed that there was no sounds being made from the thing that was on the other end of the ties. And, the faster he went the faster it went, and he decided that he was gonna run off and leave it, so he ran and it ran the same speed that he ran. And it stayed with him until he got to the east end of the Moonville Tunnel, and when he started to go into the tunnel, it went down over the hill, away from the tunnel, it didn't come into the tunnel with him."-**Interview with Clyde Pinney conducted by Kathy Simcox on Feb 23 2003**

Just over the Athens County Line—

The Devil's Tea Table
Township Hwy 21
(Kings Hollow Trail)
Nelsonville, Ohio 45764
39.327041, -82.270623

The Devil's Dance

Devil's Tea Table is off Township Hwy 21 (King Hollow Trail). It is on private property, but can be seen from the roadway.

An old legend is associated with the rock formation just over the Vinton County line into Athens County. Here is a warning—do not go there on Halloween and peer from the roadway through the trees to this unique rock caused by erosion. It was once said that at midnight on Halloween, the devil dances on top. If you see him and he looks you in the eyes, he will steal your soul!

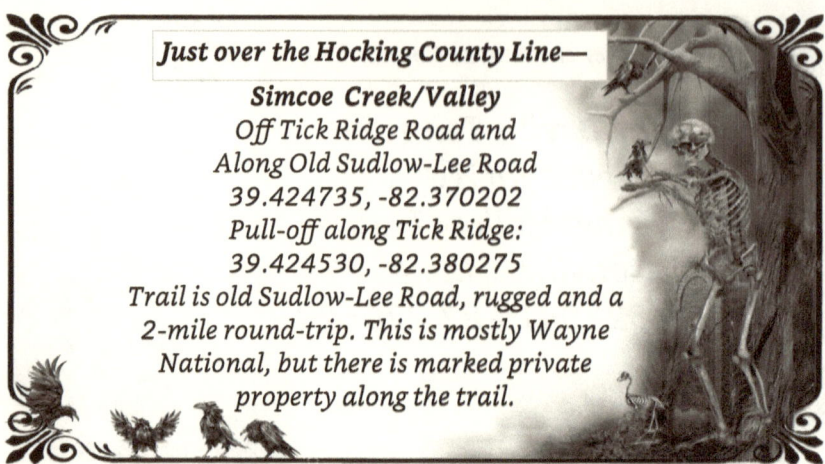

Simcoe Creek/Valley
Off Tick Ridge Road and
Along Old Sudlow-Lee Road
39.424735, -82.370202
Pull-off along Tick Ridge:
39.424530, -82.380275
Trail is old Sudlow-Lee Road, rugged and a
2-mile round-trip. This is mostly Wayne
National, but there is marked private
property along the trail.

Ghost of Simcoe Valley

Simcoe Creek and valley.

In the mid-1800s, there was a young girl named Lucille Simpson who lived on a large plantation in Virginia. Her only brother died at a young age, so her parents indulged her with nearly anything she wanted. Few children lived in the vicinity of her home, so she played almost every day with the overseer's son, Robert, who lived in a tidy cottage not far from the plantation owner's mansion.

The position of overseer had been fulfilled for many years by Robert's father, as had it been by his grandfather when Lucille's grandfather had farmed the land. As the two grew older, this friendship bloomed, and the two became secret sweethearts. Robert worked with his father during the day, managing the plantation and also ran errands for Lucille's father. Knowing his overseer's hard-working reputation and noting the son's competency, Lucille's father hired Robert as a clerk and bookkeeper in the Simpson Plantation. Robert did remarkably well, and all went smoothly until Lucille's mother began to suspect something, and upon trailing them one evening, caught them speaking sweetly together.

She brought it to her husband's attention, and the man questioned his daughter, who happily confessed the love she had for Robert and asked for her father's blessing to wed. Simpson was quite furious as he had great plans for her to marry someone of equal wealth and prominence. No child of his would marry a common hireling!

Immediately, Simpson fired both the father and the son from their household duties and barred them from his property. He prepared to send his daughter to live with relatives for a short time until things cooled between the couple. Yet, even as the Simpsons made plans to send Lucille away, she and Robert met secretly. While Lucille was out riding alone in the meadow, she was thrown from her horse one morning. It was the week of her departure to stay with an aunt, and for days she lay unconscious.

When Lucille finally awakened, it was nearly Thanksgiving, and in gratitude for his daughter's health, Simpson decided to throw a grand party. In his delight at having his daughter recover from her accident when she asked that her beloved childhood friend Robert attend, the father let his guard down and consented.

At the party, Lucille and Robert immediately found each other. Simpson was well aware of the couple chatting a little too closely, but over the week between his daughter's request to invite Robert and the night of the party, he had come up with a rather devious plan to rid his daughter of the young man once and for all. Or at least curtail the silly idea of a marriage between the two long enough he could find a more suitable match for his only child.

On that same night, he invited the couple into his office and told Robert that he would consent to a marriage on three conditions. They would postpone a wedding for exactly four years. The two could not see each other during the four years, and Robert must leave the plantation. Simpson also required that Robert make enough money to generously support Lucille by the time he returned. The old man was able to appear sincere enough about the pact that young Robert thought he just needed to prove his worth to them. Regardless, the couple had no choice but to relinquish to Lucille's father's terms.

Robert packed his bags and set off searching for a job, and a means to make his fortune. During this time, southeastern Ohio had coal, iron, and railway boomtowns due to the wealth of mineral lands. Word spread far and wide of an Englishman who decided to invest his riches on American soil and bought a great amount of land in the area around Raccoon Creek. He built many houses along soon-to-be-busy streets for workers and named the little town after himself, Zaleski. The area was flourishing in iron and coal, and the Marietta & Cincinnati railway went right through Zaleski. Robert heard of the ability to make a lot of money there and worked his way to Ohio and the budding community. When he got to Zaleski, the furnace, coal, and mining company quickly snatched him up for the bookkeeping skills he had learned under Simpson's tutelage.

For almost three years, Robert worked successfully, and his salary was plentiful. But then, Zaleski died in England, and his investments in the company town were lost. Most businesses closed, and Robert lost his job. Undaunted, the young Virginian knew that he was close to the amount of money he needed to earn to prove himself a worthy husband for Lucille. If he scrimped, found himself a meager place to stay, and worked another job, he could make up the final amount of cash to wed his sweetheart and make his way back to his home. A man named Shank would provide that income. He was a collier, a maker of charcoal for fueling the iron furnace at Union Furnace 16 miles from Zaleski. Shank was a seedy character and a known thief living in a remote area of an oak and hickory forest, which he cut to make the charcoal. Robert found work with him when it seemed scarce everywhere else after the closing of the Zaleski businesses. They lived in a dilapidated shack with another worker far outside town in a hollow with a stream, Simcoe Creek, running through it.

Union Furnace.

Making charcoal, the burned wood residue that fired the furnace, was hard and dirty work. It required cutting a large amount of timber and stacking a pile about 12 feet tall over a pit, leaving a small chimney in the center for ventilation. A worker would light the top of the chimney with burning coals from another fire. Once the pile was burning, it was covered with leaves and dirt. The woodpile would burn for about a week, leaving nothing but charcoal which was raked and allowed to cool before being loaded into wagons and taken to the furnace. But the thought of returning home to keep his pledge to his Lucille the following year kept Robert's mind occupied while he earned his meager pay. Robert would often pat the purse on his belt, which held the key to his future, smiling softly, feeling soothed with the notion he would soon be with Lucille. This habit was often observed by Shanks, who eyed the pocket hungrily.

When the time came close for the four years to end, Robert wrote to Lucille divulging that he would be home the next Thanksgiving to take her hand in marriage as he had earned enough money to seal the pact with her father. Lucille was ecstatic as she had remained true to her sweetheart, and she had begun to make arrangements to receive Robert at the plantation.

Then one dark, stormy night in mid-November, Shanks ordered Robert to go with him to tend to the midnight rounds checking to see if the charcoal pits were burning properly. Armed with shovels and lanterns, the two set off. However, only Shanks returned to the cabin. As this was not common, the other worker asked Shanks why Robert had not returned. Shanks had replied that one of the pits was not burning, so he had stayed to tend it. Robert never returned, and Shanks disappeared not long after. Most in the community thought that Shanks had murdered the young man for what he had in his purse, then threw his body into the charcoal pit.

And what became of poor Lucille? When Robert never returned, she wrote a letter to the manager of Union Furnace. He told her the awful news, yet she always believed her sweetheart was alive and would someday return. When the Civil War broke out, her father joined the southern troops. A Union soldier killed him with a bullet to the chest during a skirmish. A battle played out at the plantation, and cannons destroyed it. Having no place to go and still grieving for Robert, Lucille went to work in a hospital, fell sick, and died. Whether Lucille haunts some old, southern Civil War hospital grounds is not known. Nor do we know if her father returns to the plantation to grieve the choices he made. However, I do know the ghostly apparition of Robert is around. Travelers passing the area of the old charcoal pits in Simcoe Valley have seen a mysterious form of a man ooze up from the earth, then slowly trudge to the place where the shack belonging to Shank once stood. Then it disappears.

Simcoe Creek and valley.

Citations:

Philadelphia Inquirer) October 14, 1889: Spooks and Spirits
Athens Sunday Messenger November 10, 1963 newspaper
The Athens Asylum ballroom. Ohio University Archives, Mahn Center for Archives & Special Collections, Ohio University Libraries.
Athens Sunday Messenger November 10, 1963 Believe in the Supernatural?
-Darby, Erasmus Foster. The Ghost of Enos Kay. Chillicothe, Ohio : published privately by Dave Webb, 1953. Series: Ohio folklore series, no. 8.
-Ross County Historical Society. McKell Library, Chillicothe, Ohio.
-Athens Sunday Messenger March 11, 1923
-Republican Enquirer. (McArthur, Ohio) March 29, 1920. Vinton County. 114 Years Ago in Vinton County History, By Our Route 2 Correspondent.
Grabb, John R. The Marietta & Cincinnati railroad and its successor, the Baltimore & Ohio: a study of this once great route across Ohio, 1851-1988.
Year: 1920; Census Place: Chillicothe Ward 2, Ross, Ohio; Roll: T625_1431; Page: 15A; Enumeration District: 136
Athens Sunday Messenger August 27, 1972Price Bill. Strange Names. A Barrel. A Bog.
Bill Price. Hocking College Instructor—historical interviews.
Kathy Simcox, Historian. Interview with Clyde Pinney conducted by Kathy Simcox on Feb 23 2003
Simcoe Valley: Ohio Democrat (Logan, Oh) November 29, 1900

www.ingramcontent.com/pod-product-compliance
Lightning Source LLC
Chambersburg PA
CBHW030239180626
46810CB00008B/3206